How Giraffes Found Their Hearts

Kathleen Macferran

Art by Kenneth Schrag

ARTISAN BOOKWORKS

Story by Kathleen Macferran
Illustrations by Kenneth Schrag
Book design by Kelly Lenihan

How Giraffes Found Their Hearts/Kathleen Macferran — 1st ed.
Published 11/2021
LCCN 2019940395
ISBN 978-0991174744 (hardcover)
ISBN 978-1735789101 (softcover)

Printed in the United States of America

To my family, whom I love with all my heart.

Kathleen Macferran

To my wife, who always inspires me,
my family who nurtured what was important,
my friends who nudged me towards the right
path and connections, and those connections
who took a chance on the unknown.

Kenneth Schrag

Preface

As a music conductor, I knew the joy of children hearing stories come alive through music, yet I found few musical stories reflecting the kind of world I want to live in. Inspired by my study of Nonviolent Communication™, I decided to write children's stories, set them to music and record them as "Giraffe Tales" in the style of my earlier CD "Tales Told in the Winds."

Why giraffes? They are symbols of Nonviolent Communication since they are land animals with one of the largest hearts. When we see into each other's hearts and find out our common feelings and needs, we can transform any conflict. The giraffe also has a long neck that gives perspective about how we are interconnected and how our words, actions and thoughts impact one another. Through music and Nonviolent Communication, I've learned to listen for common ground across cultural, race, gender and age differences.

In *How the Giraffe's Got Their Ears*, the giraffes find joy when they are able to hear the beautiful feelings and needs in all hearts and empathize with each other. *How Giraffe's Found Their Hearts* is a story of the importance of being connected to our own hearts so we can live from our values and joy. Creating a world that works for all requires listening to what we cherish in life, seeing each person's dignity, empathizing with each person's experience, and acting to protect and enrich every life.

— *Kathleen Macferran*

Long, long ago, yet not so far away, giraffes were powerful beyond measure. They knew their power came from their huge hearts, from the kindness and honesty harbored there. Giraffes knew they could choose to use that power at any moment to make life wonderful for themselves and others. It was a joyful way of living.

No one knows how it happened, but slowly, very slowly, giraffes forgot about their hearts. They felt nothing stirring inside. They began to think their huge chests were empty and lifeless.

The other animals seemed to have chests filled with wonderful ticking, thumping things. Why did giraffes' chests seem so hollow? Giraffes wanted something inside that hummed and bumped too.

One day a young giraffe named Jordan decided she wanted something different. "I want life inside my empty body, but what shall I do?" she said while standing in the shade of a huge tree.

The tree heard her longing and said, "How about growing some carrots inside you? Carrots don't need much room and they are easy to grow in the richness of this earth."

"Yes!" said Jordan Giraffe, "yes, I think that's exactly what I want. I'll plant a carrot garden right now to fill up the space inside me."

Jordan Giraffe bent her long neck to the ground and began swallowing huge mouthfuls of dirt so the seeds had something in which to grow.

Next, she drank water to moisten the dirt and ate a few carrot seeds. She jumped around to mix the seeds with the soil. All the excitement made her very tired and she went to bed.

The next morning, she felt different.

"Ouch!" she said as she rolled over to get up. "Something's poking me." Then she realized the seeds had sprouted into carrots. The sharp roots were digging into her sides every time she moved.

"Oooo, my back itches like crazy," she thought. Then she rolled over to scratch her back in the dirt, she realized the carrot tops had grown right out the top of her back and were tickling her skin. "Oh, this isn't what I want," Jordan Giraffe said aloud.

So she found one of her giraffe friends to gently help pluck the carrots out. Without the carrots inside her she felt relieved, but empty again. So she set off in search of something else.

That night Jordan Giraffe couldn't sleep. She was tossing and turning, wiggling and waggling, jumping in and out of bed.

The moon noticed and said, "Jordan Giraffe, after a day of running and playing leap frog, why do you wiggle and sigh instead of sleeping like your giraffe friends?"

"Oh Moon, my chest is so empty, and I long to have something inside to fill it. Something seems to be missing. Do you know what can fill a lonely chest?" sighed Jordan Giraffe.

"Hmmmmm," murmured the moon. "The stars keep me company. They speak of things from long ago and shine like glowing campfires throughout the night. How about filling your chest with the quiet of the night sky?"

"Yes! That is what I'll do! Maybe this emptiness can be filled with the light of the stars."

So Jordan Giraffe took a deep, long breath, opening her mouth wide to let the stars in. As they slid down her throat, she felt icy air and cool silence fill her body.

"Now I am full and can sleep," she thought. With her chest filled with stars, Jordan Giraffe fell asleep.

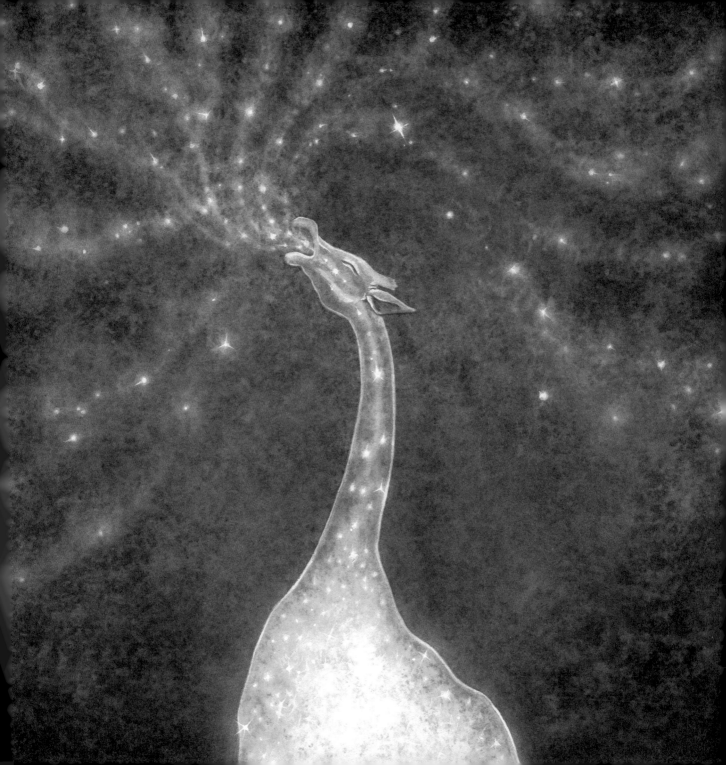

During the next several days and nights, Jordan Giraffe wandered slowly.

The rising sun in the mornings warmed her body and she felt content. In the evenings she enjoyed the glowing of starlight and the peacefulness of the vast space.

Yet, having so much space inside her made it difficult to feel close to her giraffe friends. Her thoughts seemed far away.

Jordan Giraffe longed to laugh and run with the giraffes again. It seemed difficult now, as if she lived in a different world.

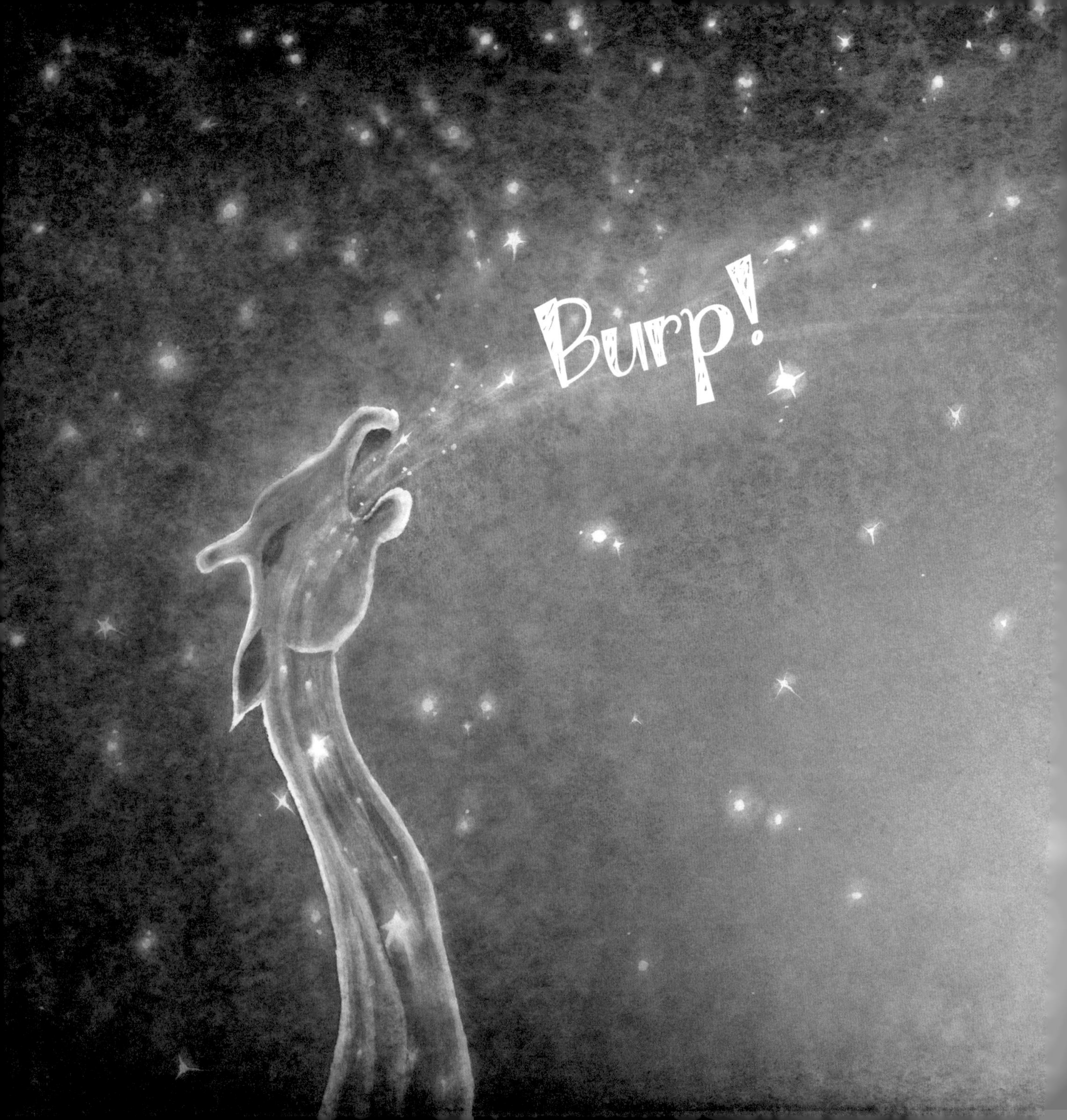
Burp!

"I miss playing with my friends," sighed Jordan Giraffe. "Tonight I will give the stars back to the sky." She opened her mouth and gently released her breath, returning all of the stars to the night sky.

Out flew a shooting star. Jordan Giraffe made a wish on the last star to leave, wishing for something to fill her chest.

Several days later, Jordan Giraffe wandered near a small pond, peaceful like the stars, yet so full of life. There were frogs, salamanders, and fish zooming around plants, splashing in the water, and shivering with excitement.

"Oh Pond, you seem so happy here, surrounded by friends, full of life. I'm empty inside and I'm hoping you can suggest something to put in my chest so I can be full of life, too," said Jordan Giraffe.

The pond thought for a minute and said, "The water provides a home for all living things here. How about filling your chest with water and all the wonderful animals and plants that live there?"

"Oh, thank you, Pond! I will do that. Surely I will be happy then."

So Jordan Giraffe took a long, very long drink until she was completely full of water. Along her ribs she could feel fish swimming, salamanders crawling, and frogs jumping.

Having all this inside was so exciting.

"I must tell the other giraffes," she thought. Jordan Giraffe started walking home.

A huge wave swelled inside her and threw her off balance.

Down she fell on her nose. The water inside was rocking her back and forth from side to side as she was lying on the ground. She couldn't get up. She remained perfectly still breathing in the scent of wildflowers for what seemed like hours until the calm returned.

The water was lovely as long as she didn't move, but how was she going to get around? She tried to get up again, but the swishing of the water threw her back on her side.

"Oh, well," thought Jordan Giraffe. "I guess the water will need to stay here in the pond."

Then she blew a gentle breath across the surface of the water until the waves tumbled into a waterfall down her tongue, through a hollow log near her head and back to the ground.

Feeling discouraged,
Jordan Giraffe walked home.

As the days passed, Jordan Giraffe was losing hope of finding anything to fill her hollow chest. She started to cry giant, giraffe-sized tears.

Then faintly in the distance, she heard singing that reminded her of the light from the stars, the joy of the pond, the richness of the earth and the scent of wildflowers.

Jordan Giraffe dried her tears and started walking in the direction of the song. As she walked on, the song grew louder and more inviting, drawing her closer.

After journeying for many miles, Jordan Giraffe saw who was making the sound. A small boy was singing while drawing pictures with sticks in the dirt.

Feeling a little shy, yet wanting to be near the boy, Jordan Giraffe inched forward.

"Hi. I'm hoping you might be willing to help me. Inside my chest there is a big hollow space that seems so empty. When I heard your song, I thought maybe a song is what I want to fill my empty space. Do you think you could tell me where to get a song?"

The boy looked straight into Jordan Giraffe's eyes and smiled. Jordan Giraffe was amazed to see such kindness and joy coming from the eyes of someone so young.

The boy said, "My song comes from the heart that grows inside my chest. Every time I sing, my heart grows a little larger. Perhaps it is a large heart that you seek."

Jordan Giraffe was quiet for a long time, looking at the boy with curiosity. As the boy looked back, Jordan Giraffe felt warmth in the middle of her chest. It began to fill her whole body and a smile spread on her lips. Yes, it was a heart she was looking for.

Eagerly she asked the boy, "Please, tell me how I can get a heart with a song as beautiful as yours!"

The boy smiled.
"Just listen.
Close your eyes
and listen."

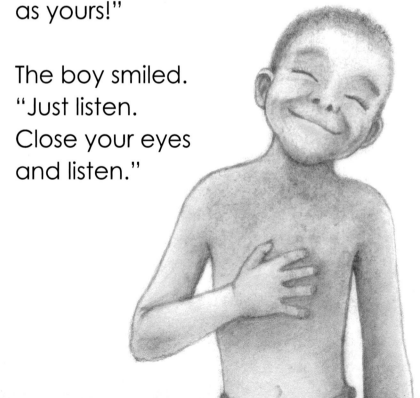

Jordan Giraffe closed her eyes and listened as hard as she could. She listened to the space beyond the stars. She listened below the roots of the wildflowers. She listened to the moonbeams, the waves, and the sunlight.

Then she heard something new, something so quiet she had to stand absolutely still to hear it. Even though it seemed new, it was also something she recognized from long ago. Why, she knew this song very well—the shape of its line, even the color of the pauses was familiar.

The boy laughed when he saw the happy look on Jordan Giraffe's face. He said,

"You are hearing your own song, aren't you? Your heart has been there all along. Now you've found it again. Every time you sing your song, your heart will grow. Every time you cry, tears will water your heart, washing it clean and letting it drink when it is thirsty. Every time you laugh, your heart will be fed and satisfied."

Jordan Giraffe knew her search was over. Her heart had been there all along.

She was so happy to discover it again that she watered and fed it every day with tears and laughter. She sang its song to everyone she met.

Soon, Jordan Giraffe had the largest heart of all living animals on land. She sang with joy and listened to the songs of the other giraffes so they could remember their hearts too.

Today giraffes still walk the earth, but their chests no longer seem empty. Giraffes have found their powerful hearts once again and, in harmony, sing their songs of life.

Thank you for adding
How Giraffes Found Their Hearts
to your library.

If your child enjoyed this story, please consider
posting a thoughtful review on Amazon or other
favorite book site on your child's behalf.

Your kindness will make a difference
for others considering this book.

Please note, the second book in the Giraffe series, *How Giraffes Got Their Ears* is available upon request from your favorite bookseller or library. Just ask for ISBN 978-0991174751 (hardcover).

The Giraffe series is also available in ebook format. Visit StrengthofConnection.com for details on the ebooks, "Giraffe Tales" audio download of music and narration, "Tales Told in the Winds" audio download, and other books by Kathleen.

Meet the Author

I dream of a world that works—really works—for all. My plan is to use my remaining days to make that a reality, to find ways to hear marginalized voices, to bring equitable access to our resources, to celebrate our diverse and miraculous world.

Kathleen Macferran

To find out more about Kathleen, view her TEDx talks, and discover where she is offering workshops and projects around the world, visit StrengthofConnection.com.

Meet the Illustrator

Essentially, I am still just another kid that likes to draw pictures, and I hope that others might find joy in, have an emotional connection to, or are inspired by some of the images that spill out of my head.

Kenneth Schrag

To find out more about Kenneth, visit kennethschrag.com.

Acknowledgments

So many colleagues came together to make this book and music possible: Kenneth Schrag who brought the story alive with his dynamic illustrations, Adam Stern who created a musical landscape for the characters to breathe their first breaths, the narrators and Rainier Chamber Winds' musicians who put flesh and bones on the story. I am thankful to Kelly Lenihan for her endless patience bringing this book to life and Artisan Bookworks whose design and marketing expertise have been indispensable. Deep bows to all of you. I'm humbled by the power of your art and believe the world is a magical place because of you.

To my daughters, Kayla and Jordan, thank you for exploring the land of giraffes with me. Your big hearts and wisdom have taught me much and made my life richer.

Finally, I'm grateful to my teacher, Marshall B. Rosenberg, founder of Nonviolent Communication™, who traveled the world sharing his wisdom about how we could get along with one another. His ideas shaped these stories. That legacy is carried on today by every person who stands for the rights and well-being of all. To every one of you, I thank you. You have my deepest respect and gratitude.

— *Kathleen Macferran*

Made in the USA
Coppell, TX
17 June 2023

18184698R00033